Roland Wright
Future Knight

Don't miss these great books!

Roland Wright

#1 *Future Knight*

And coming soon

#2 *Brand-New Page*

Roland Wright
Future Knight

by Tony Davis

illustrated by Gregory Rogers

Delacorte Press

All rights reserved. Published in the United States by Delacorte Press, an imprint of Random House Children's Books, a division of Random House, Inc., New York. Originally published in paperback by Random House Australia, Sydney, in 2007.

Delacorte Press is a registered trademark and the colophon is a trademark of Random House, Inc.

Visit us on the Web! www.randomhouse.com/kids

Educators and librarians, for a variety of teaching tools, visit us at www.randomhouse.com/teachers

Library of Congress Cataloging-in-Publication Data
Davis, Tony.
Future knight / by Tony Davis ; illustrated by Gregory Rogers. — 1st American ed.
p. cm. — (Roland Wright ; #1)
Summary: In 1409, skinny, clumsy Roland, the ten-year-old son of a blacksmith, pursues his dream of becoming a knight.
ISBN: 978-0-385-73800-2 (hc)—ISBN: 978-0-385-90706-4 (glb)—
ISBN: 978-0-375-89403-9 (e-book)
[1. Knights and knighthood—Fiction. 2. Middle Ages—Fiction.]
I. Rogers, Gregory, ill. II. Title.
PZ7.D3194Fu 2009
[Fic]—dc22
2008053074

The text of this book is set in 16-point Bembo.
Book design by Michelle Gengaro

Printed in the United States of America

10 9 8 7 6 5 4 3 2 1

First American Edition

Contents

Roland Wright
Future Knight

One

Something Special

These days it is considered rude to chop a man's arm off with a battle-axe, even when you don't like him.

And when someone is *really* annoying, or is standing in your way and will not move, it is not polite to take a large silver sword and swing it with all your force at eye level, neatly removing the top of that person's head.

But it wasn't always like that.

Six centuries ago, a boy named Roland

Wright turned ten. Well, nearly ten. It was the year 1409, in a period known as the Middle Ages. Almost everything was different from the way it is today.

For a start, there were no cars. There were no planes either. Television? Not even in black-and-white.

Books had to be written out by hand because the man who was going to invent printing wasn't even a teenager yet.

People went from one place to another by foot or, if they were very lucky, by horse. But even traveling by horse wasn't easy or comfortable. The roads of the Middle Ages were made of dirt, and the dirt was dirtier than it is today. When it rained the roads turned to mud, and the mud was muddier too.

Most people lived in the country, not in cities. The houses in Roland's village had roofs made of straw, and no chimneys. All through winter they were full of smoke because the only way to heat them was to light a fire inside. The only way to cool houses in summer was to open a window, and the windows were made of wood.

Worse still, many families had to share their house with their animals, particularly when it was cold or wet. Everything would smell of pig and donkey and chicken, except for pigs and donkeys and chickens, which probably smelled of house.

Life in the Middle Ages wasn't only tough and a bit pongy, it could also be pretty danger-ous. Many arguments, large and small, were sorted out by knights in armor fighting each other with large and terrible weapons.

Sometimes they used huge broadswords, sharp

on both sides and capable of slicing a tree in two. They had big ugly maces too, with a long handle and a metal ball at the end covered with horrible spikes. When the mace was swung hard enough, these spikes could even puncture armor.

Some knights had long poleaxes, or spears. These were so pointy that they could poke right through somcone's body, causing blood to squirt out both sides like tomato sauce squirts out of those little plastic-and-foil tubs that you turn upside down over a meat pie and bend in half.

Of course, arguments in 1409 were not always sorted out in such a way.

Jenny Winterbottom, who lived near Roland Wright in a small white house at the edge of the woods, said that birds could fly because they weighed less than clouds.

Roland knew this wasn't right. But he didn't grab his big, spiky steel mace and hit her over the head so hard that her brain shot out her earholes like lengths of gray rope.

He simply said, "No, they don't. You are wrong."

"I am not," Jenny said. Her brown curls swung as she spoke. "And you're stupid."

No boy who is almost ten likes being called stupid, especially by a girl who is only just nine and has curly hair. But Roland still didn't grab his big, spiky steel mace with both hands and bring it down

like a sledgehammer over her forehead.

This was because Roland quite liked Jenny and was happy to play with her, as long as there was no one else around. It was also because he didn't have the slightest idea why birds could fly either.

Roland thought it had something to do with the feathers. However, when he tied a pile of feathers to Nudge, his pet white mouse, Nudge just curled up and looked sad.

Even throwing Nudge into the air didn't seem to help him fly. He came down at exactly the same speed as he would have without feathers. And Nudge was very lucky the ground was there to stop him, otherwise he would have kept falling.

There was one other reason Roland didn't clout Jenny Winterbottom over the head. Like many people named Jenny, she was a girl.

In the time of knights and armor, some men could be very nasty and cruel to other men. But they all tried as hard as they could to be nice to women.

There were lots of stories of men slaying dragons to rescue fair maidens. This sounded very exciting to Roland. But there were also stories of men taking off their coats and laying them over puddles, so women could walk without splashing any yucky mud on their dainty boots. That didn't sound like nearly as much fun as slaying dragons.

Behaving like this was called chivalry. Roland thought this might be because if you took off your coat on a cold day you would start chivering. Then again, Roland couldn't spell.

Anyway, for all that, Roland didn't have a spiky steel mace. He had only a small wooden one that he had made himself out of a stick and a round knob of wood from a tree root.

Roland wasn't allowed to have a real mace because Roland wasn't a knight.

Roland wasn't even a page, which is what you had to be before you were a squire, which was what you had to be before you were a knight. And a knight was what you had to be if you wanted to carry around a real mace and swing it at people who annoyed you.

Still, Roland loved fighting with a wooden sword, and Shelby, his older, bigger, stronger brother, had to work harder and harder to beat him.

When they were swinging their wooden swords a few days earlier, Roland stuck out his bottom lip, like he always did when he was trying hard. He thrust and lunged and swiped, hitting Shelby's sword so hard it flew out of his hand.

"Ouch," shouted Shelby, who could usually move more quickly than Roland. "That's not fair!"

"Yes, it is fair," said Roland. "Now, yield, Sir Shelby. Yield to Roland Wright— future knight."

"All right, I yield," Shelby said, falling to his knees and holding up his hands. "But you know as well as I do that you can never really be a knight. Only the children of the rich and noble become knights."

"I'm going to fight so well, they'll have to make me a knight," said Roland.

"What rot!" said Shelby. "That's not how it works. The only thing certain is that in our family I am the oldest son, so I will take over the family business. You'll have to work for me, Roland, and I'll give you the worst job I can find."

Roland lifted his sword high above his head.

"I should cut you in two, Sir Shelby," Roland said. "Or three, or four, or five. I should slice off your ears and carve up your gizzards. But I am a good knight, so I will show mercy."

Just as Roland was speaking, Shelby leapt to his feet and ran for his sword.

"So," said Shelby, picking up his wooden broadsword and swinging it wildly, "if you are a good knight, then it's good night to you."

Shelby laughed loudly at his trickery.

"That's not right," yelled Roland. "When a true knight yields, he gives his word. You'll have to die for that!"

Straightaway, the whole fight started again.

Shelby was a year and a half older than Roland, but, like his brother, Shelby couldn't spell, read or write.

They couldn't spell, read or write

because there were hardly any schools in the whole country. Anyway, there was no time for sitting in classrooms because in the Middle Ages most children were expected to work.

Roland and Shelby's father, Oliver Wright, had been trained as a blacksmith from the time he was a young boy. He could spell out no more than his name. He had never even seen a book other than the handwritten Bible that the priest read from in the village church. And that was in Latin.

That's not to say the Wrights weren't smart. They were very smart indeed. And on one late summer afternoon in 1409, Roland sensed that he and Shelby were about to be given an amazing chance to prove it.

"Something special is going to happen, Nudge," Roland said as he sat in the fork of his favorite oak tree. When Roland was excited, Nudge would usually be standing on his rear legs, peering at the horizon with his black eyes, sniffing the air with his twitchy pink nose.

But since his flying lesson, Nudge had been very quiet and still.

"Flaming catapults, Nudge, I can just feel it," Roland said. "When I go to the forge this afternoon I'm going to have my hair brushed and my Sunday clothes on. I don't know what it is, but it's something big."

"   ," said Nudge, who couldn't talk because he was a mouse.

Even if Nudge had been able to talk, he would have had no wish to do so today. He had a huge headache and blamed Roland.

Two

The Forge

With Nudge's white face peering out the top of his shirt pocket, Roland walked through the cornfield toward the village square and his father's forge, or metalworks.

The path was bumpy and narrow. Roland could smell the heavy corn and knew they would be cutting it any day. He could see Farmer Jones leading a large cow toward him.

"Morning, Master Roland. Lovely August day, isn't it?"

"Yes it is, Mr. Jones," said Roland as he squeezed sideways past the huge animal. Roland heard the church bells ring and realized he was late for work. He started to jog.

Roland had a red tinge to his hair, a rash of freckles across his nose and cheeks, and was small for his age.

He was thin, too—so skinny he looked as though a decent wind could snap him in two. But Roland could eat more than just about any grown-up. And what he lacked in size he more than made up for in heart.

Now Roland crossed the cobblestones of the village square and arrived at the forge. His hair was brushed. He had pulled up around his ears the collar of his Sunday tunic, the only spare piece of clothing Roland owned. His leather belt was polished and pulled tight. The metal buckles on his shoes were shining.

The forge was huge and dark, like a barn. Inside, there was a red glow from the smith's furnace, the big fire in the middle where the metal was heated.

The smith's furnace spat out sparks and smoke as it roared and flickered. On a day like today Roland sweated from the

moment he arrived, but when it was snowing outside there was nowhere better to be.

The forge seemed to be bigger and busier every day. When Roland was younger, his father worked alone in a small shed. He made horseshoes. Then he discovered there was something he could do much better.

Now, above the main door was a big painted sign that showed a knight in gleaming armor lifting a sword above his head. You didn't need to be able to read the letters below the sign—W–R–I–G–H–T— to know that this was where Oliver Wright made his famous armor.

People worked in every corner. Roland stopped and said hello to Old Tobias and his young apprentice, David. Old Tobias ran the furnace and supplied the wrought iron for all the other workers.

Neither seemed to notice Roland. David blew air onto the fire with large leather bellows, which made it rain sparks

all through the forge. When the fire was as hot as it could be, Old Tobias used long tongs to put in a big lump of metal.

Roland knew Old Tobias would take this lump out when it was so hot it glowed red. Old Tobias and David would then beat it against an iron anvil with large mallets. It was such noisy work that Old Tobias had completely lost his hearing. Already David's favorite word was "what?"

In other places there were hammerers

beating sheets of steel into shape. There were millmen polishing newly made helmets and breastplates and shields.

There were locksmiths working on hinges and joints. But one thing was very different from most other places where armor was made: there were no engravers scraping fancy patterns into the metal. Mr. Wright liked his armor very simple.

Roland stood looking at Mr. Nottingham, the mail-maker. Mr. Nottingham was locking rings of wire together to make a "cloth" of metal. He was counting the rows as if he was knitting a steel jumper.

"What is that, Mr. Nottingham?" Roland asked above the din of the hammering and pounding and thumping.

"It's for an 'orse, Master Roland. A suit of mail to protect an 'orse. We call it a barde. I started yesterday and reckon I'll have this section finished within six weeks."

Roland looked at Mr. Nottingham's work with wonder. Roland imagined himself in full armor, riding into battle on a magnificent warhorse covered with a shining barde.

The hammering in the forge became the noise of arrows bouncing off Roland's suit of steel. The yelling became the sound of the enemy retreating as Roland swung his broadsword and yelled, "Death to the traitors!"

After a short daydream, Roland returned to the real world, which was a fair bit less interesting. He walked up to see what his brother was doing.

Now that he was eleven years old, Shelby worked at the forge all of every day except Sunday, because that was the Lord's day and nobody in the village worked on Sunday. They prayed and went to Mass, then ate a big Sunday meal.

After that, the girls danced and did boring girl things while the boys kicked around a pig's bladder filled with air, or fought battles against each other with their wooden weapons.

This afternoon Shelby was dropping oil onto the hinges of a new suit of armor. The armor glimmered with the flashing fire-light, and shone whenever fine rays of sun snuck in through the gaps in the straw roof.

"Is something important happening today?" whispered Roland.

"I don't think so," said Shelby

with a shrug. Shelby was taller than Roland, with a heavier frame and hair so blond it glowed even in the darkness of the forge. "Is this another one of your stupid hunches . . . is that why you have your Sunday tunic on?"

"Yes," said Roland as Shelby turned back to his work. "But I think this hunch is right. All day I've had a feeling something very special is going to happen."

"What rot!"

The armor that Shelby was now oiling had taken half the year to finish, even though there were several people working on it. It had 150 separate parts but looked simple and strong, and was beautifully made. Most importantly, it was plate armor.

Plate armor was a complete suit of hard steel that covered a knight from top to toe. Roland and Shelby's father was famous in the whole region because he was the first to make it.

Before, armor had been made of separate

pieces of steel connected by mail. Plate armor was stronger and meant a knight could fight in battle without a shield, knowing the suit would protect him. Plate armor could be made only by a tradesman as clever and skillful as Oliver Wright.

Many people wanted to buy it. People had said Mr. Wright should move his business to the city, but he had simply said: "If they want it, they can come here to get it."

There were even stories that the King had ordered a suit, secretly sending a young knight who was exactly the same size so that all the measurements could be taken and the armor made to fit.

The knight had paid the bill and taken the suit away nearly six months later. But nothing more had been heard.

That didn't stop Roland daydreaming about King John setting off to conquer new lands in a suit of Wright plate armor. Roland was by his side to protect the King, slay the enemy and even chop the occasional fire-breathing dragon into little bits.

As for any fair maidens . . . well, if they liked climbing trees and hunting with slingshots, he just might rescue them. But he wasn't putting his Sunday tunic on the muddy ground for anyone.

Sadly, though, boys such as Roland were almost never trained to be pages, squires or knights. For a start, their families couldn't afford it. It cost an enormous amount of money to equip a knight, not only with armor but with horses and weapons and a squire to help him.

It was so unfair. Roland was sure he would be the best knight in the world. For hours on end he threw an acorn against the wall of the village well and slashed at it with his wooden sword when it bounced back.

An oval-shaped acorn hitting a curved wall could go in any direction, but Roland could hit it almost every time.

Whenever Shelby saw his younger

brother with his sword and acorn, he just laughed. "That's such a stupid thing to do, Roland. You are either born strong and quick like me, or you are born slow and clumsy like you. And if you are born slow and clumsy, nothing will ever make you a good swordsman. And you look silly with your bottom lip sticking out."

Roland shook his head and realized he was daydreaming again. He wasn't in far-off lands fighting dragons or even outside hitting acorns. He wasn't arguing with his brother, or fighting him with his sword and shield. He was at his father's forge, and he was supposed to be working. He heard Shelby talking nearby.

"Leave me alone, Roland, and attend to your own little jobs. Unlike you, I have important things to do."

Roland didn't move. In his mind he was now using his shield to block the fire coming out of a large green dragon's mouth. He was waiting until the dragon ran out of breath so he could jump out from behind his shield and stab it in the heart.

"Stop daydreaming!" yelled Shelby, who was now very angry. "I am going to be your boss one day, Roland, so you should get used to me giving you orders. Here's one right now: GO AWAY!"

Roland walked a few paces toward a full suit of armor laid out on a workbench. The helmet was resting on an anvil. It was an old-fashioned suit of armor and very battered. Suddenly Roland realized there was a moaning noise coming from within. The moaning grew louder.

Roland's father appeared and spoke to the suit of armor in his slow, deep voice.

"Wait there, sir," said Oliver Wright. "I have to find the right device to hit your head."

Three

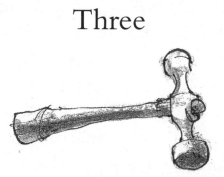

Sir Gallawood

"Oooohhhh," the knight in the battered armor moaned.

"Ooooohhhh," he moaned again, adding another "Ooooohhhh" almost straightaway.

Roland stepped closer as the moaning knight lay there waiting for Mr. Wright to return with the right device to hit him on the head.

"What happened, sir?" Roland asked the knight. Roland had forgotten what his father had told him: that a young boy should never speak to an adult unless spoken to. He certainly shouldn't start a conversation with a nobleman.

"Ooooohhhh. I was in a joust, a friendly joust at the Queen's Festival," said the knight from beneath his squashed visor. "And—ooooohhhh—I was hit in the chest by my opponent's lance."

The knight had a low, unhappy voice that sounded like it was coming out of a long tunnel.

"And as I fell off my horse I hit the barrier and then got kicked by my own steed, which was all in a panic. Ooooohhhh.

"My visor spun around and I could no longer see out. For the first time in my career I had to yield. I had to give up.

"Ooooohhhh, and if that wasn't bad enough, I couldn't get my head out of my squashed helmet. Even my own blacksmith couldn't get it out."

Mr. Wright came over with a large flat-headed hammer. "This should prove suitable, sir."

Roland's father had such a deep voice that the visor on the knight's helmet rattled when he spoke. Mr. Wright lifted his arm high and started pounding the helmet back into shape.

Bang. "Ouch."

Thump. "Ooooow."

Thud. "Yeeeeps."

Wallop. "Ooooohhhh."

With a final sigh, which sounded exactly halfway between an "aaaaaahh" and an "eeeeerrrrr," the knight jumped to his feet. He lifted the reshaped helmet off his head and stuck his fingers into his ears.

"Sorry about the yelling, my good man," he finally said, looking down at Mr.

Wright, who was much shorter. "It's not really the knightly thing to do. But it's a bit loud inside a metal helmet when someone is hitting it with a hammer. My ears are chiming like church bells. But I'm most appreciative, my good man, thank you."

Roland's father didn't say anything. He never said too much, and when he did, he tended to use many of the big words he picked up from the knights who bought his armor. Some of these words were very substantial, extended and elongated. Yet Roland and Shelby always seemed to know what he meant.

This time Mr. Wright just nodded at the knight, then walked away to put his hammer back in the toolbox.

The knight's head was horribly bruised and he had blood on his cheeks. But Roland saw his long black hair and pointy beard and knew straightaway who the knight was.

"Sir Gallawood," Roland yelled out. He had again forgotten he had no right to speak to a knight. "I'm Roland Wright— Oliver's son—and I'm so happy to meet you. You are my favorite knight. I think you are the best fighter of them all."

"Oh, why is that?" Sir Gallawood asked as he rubbed his swollen ears.

Roland was so excited he was talking at twice his normal speed.

"You are the best fighter, not just because you live at the castle near our village. No, no, no. It's because of the way you move quickly and tire out the other knights. You are so much fitter than they

are and stronger, too. And I like the way
you keep trying, no matter what happens."

"I don't think I was the best fighter
today," Sir Gallawood said softly. "But I'm
very pleased to meet you too, young man.

I've heard that your father is the most skillful armorer in the land."

Sir Gallawood rubbed his face, then twisted his fingers in his ears.

"I'm lucky I wasn't killed today, so I won't be using any more of the armor passed on from my father. I always thought that if I was a good enough fighter, the type of armor didn't matter. But now I will order a set of Wright plate armor."

Roland beamed with pride. He was sure he could feel Nudge in his top pocket wriggling with pride too.

"I think my father is the greatest armorer in the land too," Roland said. "It's not just that he makes plate armor. He says metal with scrolls and frills might look fancy, but it isn't as strong."

Roland talked even more quickly. "Metal with scrolls and frills isn't as light either. Father says you have to build armor for strength, not style. And it has to bend easily at the joints so that you can move quickly. And the weight has to be spread evenly.

"Knights wearing my father's armor can do somersaults and run almost as fast as a man in normal clothes."

"I see," Sir Gallawood said to Roland with a smile. "Oliver Wright will never have trouble selling his armor with a son like you, now will he?"

As he said the words "now will he?" Sir Gallawood let out a loud laugh. He then gave Roland a friendly punch on the shoulder. The power of Sir Gallawood's huge fist—even in play—knocked Roland two steps sideward.

At that exact moment, a group of six men in uniform appeared in the main doorway. They wore long, bright red coats and tall black boots. They had big floppy hats on their heads and frilly white scarves around their necks. They stood in two rows and played a short tune with their long trumpets.

Everyone in the forge put down their tools and walked toward the door. For once the factory was silent, except for the crackle and roar of the smith's furnace.

The workers at the forge had never seen anything quite like it. Not in this small village, anyway. Colorful clothes needed rare and costly dyes; large leather boots took months to make. Yet here were six men

dressed in the finest uniforms the workers had ever seen, each carrying an expensive brass instrument.

A seventh man suddenly walked between the trumpeters. He was dressed in an even longer and fancier red coat. His flat black hat was even bigger and was topped with a plume made of white silk.

He started to talk in a voice as loud as thunder.

"As a herald of the royal castle . . . ," he bellowed.

Roland could feel Nudge push himself deeply into the corner of his shirt pocket as the man spoke. Roland ran his finger gently over Nudge's back and whispered to him, "Don't worry, he says he is from the royal castle. I think it's good news. I think I was right, something special is happening."

"I hereby announce," the herald continued, "that His Majesty's officer-of-arms is coming with an important message directly from the King for Mr. Oliver Wright. He will arrive shortly."

Four

The Greatest Day

At exactly "shortly," the entire staff of Oliver Wright's armor factory was still standing and waiting in stunned silence.

No one in the village had ever before come so close to anyone so close to the King. Except perhaps for the knight who was sent to purchase the King's armor. But he had hardly said a word—and maybe that was just a story. Maybe he had nothing to do with the royal family.

This was different: the beautifully clean uniforms, the rare sound of trumpets, and the chance to see and hear King John's own officer-of-arms.

At shortly and a half, a large, bearded man walked past the herald and through the two rows of trumpeters. His tabard, or sleeveless coat, was covered in big swirls of gold embroidery. On the front and back was the royal coat of arms.

Roland wouldn't have believed anyone could have a louder voice than the herald of the royal castle. But the officer-of-arms did. He held a long scroll of paper and proclaimed in a beautifully clear but horribly loud voice: "Hear ye, hear ye, hear ye!"

"Why does he repeat himself?" Roland asked his brother. "We heard him loudly enough the first time."

"Be quiet," said Shelby. "That's the way they say it to make it important and official."

"Hear ye, hear ye, hear ye!" the officer-of-arms said again. "His Majesty King John has sent me on his behalf to convey a message to Mr. Oliver Wright. The message is this: In the recent Battle of Two Tree Hill, your King again fought bravely and nobly for his subjects, riding with the front line. During the fight he was struck in the shoulder by a poisoned bolt fired from a crossbow.

"The bolt hit the joint, the place where

armor is normally the weakest. But it did not pierce the steel.

"After the battle was won, the King asked his blacksmiths to look at his suit of armor, stamped with the simple imprint 'Wright.' They said what saved His Majesty's life was the simple, strong design and the fact that it was plate steel all over."

Roland gasped. So it was true. The King did have a set of his father's armor. The officer-of-arms kept talking.

"His Majesty would like to convey his gratitude to the maker of this armor. What is more, the King wishes to show this gratitude. He will do this in two important ways. Firstly, by allowing Mr. Oliver Wright to stamp on all the armor he makes the words 'By Royal Appointment.'"

Roland turned to Shelby. "'By Royal Appointment.' That's going to be hard to spell."

"Quiet!" snapped Shelby.

"Secondly," the officer-of-arms continued, "he has learned that Mr. Oliver Wright has two sons. His Majesty will take one of these two sons into the royal household to be trained as a page.

"It is a great honor for the son who is chosen, and the King is sure that if the son has the qualities of his father, he will not let His Majesty down."

Roland started shaking with excitement.

"Flaming catapults, Nudge," he whispered to his top pocket. "I can't believe this, and I am sure you can't either. This means I will become a page. And if I become a page, Nudge, I can become a squire. And if I can become a squire, I can become a knight. And if I can become a knight I will get a real suit of armor, a real warhorse, a real lance for jousting and a real-life, big, spiky steel mace."

The officer-of-arms continued talking, but Roland was no longer listening. He was too busy thinking how proud he was of his father, and how proud his father would be when Roland learned to read, to hunt with falcons, to play a musical instrument, to ride a horse and to do all the other things a page was taught to do.

"This is the most important day of my life, Nudge," he whispered. "I will learn all about swords and longbows and crossbows and all sorts of other weapons. And you will come with me!"

Then Roland looked across the forge and saw his brother. "We're just lucky, Nudge, that Shelby is going to take over the business."

Roland looked through the doorway to see that many people from the village had walked across the square to see what the hullabaloo was about. Farmer Jones was there with his cow, and Jenny Winterbottom was there with her mother, who always wore a white wimple and smelled strongly of lavender. Mrs. Winterbottom had large eyes and a sharp, pointy nose like a sparrow hawk. She looked at everything now happening in front of her and started shaking her head and saying "Dear, dear, dear."

The final words of the officer-of-arms were: "Now the King orders you all to feast," and with that he turned and left the forge, followed by the herald and the six trumpeters.

Suddenly four men in white uniforms climbed out of a tall brown wagon that had appeared in the village square. They carried a large cooked animal on a round silver tray.

The animal was roasted to a golden brown color, and was the strangest thing that Roland had ever seen. It had a head and shoulders like a rooster but the body of a piglet. It also had small wings, still covered in feathers.

"A flying pig?" Roland couldn't believe it. He turned to Shelby. "A capon with the body of a hog? Where does such a beast live?"

"You fool," said Shelby. "It's a cockentrice. It's what rich people eat. Cooks take half of one creature and sew it to half of another to make a pretend new animal. They mix all the meat together and stuff it and roast it."

"How do you know these things?" asked Roland.

"Older brothers know everything."

The workers began to clap and cheer Oliver Wright, while the chefs sliced their creation.

"Bravo, good 'ealth to you, Mr. Wright," yelled Mr. Nottingham, the mail-maker. It was a bit hard to understand him, though. His mouth was already filled with roostig—or was it pigster?

"And I should add that I've never tasted meat 'alf as rich as this," Mr. Nottingham spluttered, "with so many fruits and 'erbs and spices in it too."

Just as Mr. Nottingham spoke, Roland felt his father's big powerful arm wrap around his shoulder. He looked up to see Shelby under his father's other arm. Mr. Wright, who so rarely showed his feelings, was smiling what for most people would be a small smile. But it was the biggest smile that his sons had ever seen Mr. Wright smile.

"Well done, everybody," said Mr. Wright. "It is an immense honor. But we all make the armor together, so it is something we can all be proud of. And those of you who haven't already partaken of the cockentrice, please do so."

Sir Gallawood, who had waited around to hear the officer-of-arms, began clapping again at the end of Mr. Wright's short speech.

"Already I have a second reason to say well done, my good man," Sir Gallawood said. He then turned to the crowd and said in a large, knightly voice: "It is a wonderful thing to save a king."

Sir Gallawood lifted his repaired helmet back onto his head. He jumped onto his horse, lifted his visor and looked straight at Oliver Wright and his two sons. "And if there is anything I can do to help any of you, let me know."

"How about not punching me again," thought Roland, but he didn't say it out loud. He liked Sir Gallawood even more now that he had met him, and anyway, this was the greatest day of Roland's life. What did a sore shoulder matter?

When Sir Gallawood rode off, Mr. Wright

turned to Roland, who was now trying to see how much cockentrice he could fit into his mouth. Mr. Wright's smile was gone. He was back to his usual self.

"Well, that's enough exhilaration for now," said Mr. Wright. "Eat up nice and quick. And make sure your friend Jenny gets some too."

"She's not my friend," said Roland. "She's our neighbor."

"Well, either way, it's a busy day, son."

"But can't we talk, Father, can't we talk?" Roland was almost shrieking with excitement. His father's eyes seemed to move closer together and his forehead scrunched up. It was the Look. Without words, the Look said that there was going to be no more talking from Roland and a lot more working.

"You can start, Roland, by bringing in the coal. Then you can sweep up the metal filings so we can reuse them. And when Shelby has accomplished his tasks, then I'll sit you both down and explain what we should do about King John's offer."

Roland already knew what they should do. They should say "Yes" straightaway and send Roland directly to the royal household. As he carried in the big lumps of coal needed to keep the smith's furnace burning and stacked them high, Roland thought of nothing else.

"Isn't it wonderful?" he said to Shelby, who had gone back to oiling hinges. "I'm going to be the best page in the world, then the best squire, then the best knight."

Shelby looked up with surprise and anger. "You? *You?* What do you mean *you?*"

"Well, you are going to take over the armor business, like you always say, and I—"

"That was then," sneered Shelby. "Now everything has changed. I'm the oldest, I'm better at doing things. So it will be me, not you, Roland, who will live at the King's castle. It will be me who will eat a whole cockentrice at supper every night—and it will be me who will sleep on a bed of softest duck feathers."

Five

The Decision

The working day was over, and Roland and Shelby were sitting in the forge. Each was holding a bowl of pottage that their father had heated up over the smith's furnace.

For once Roland wasn't scoffing his supper and straightaway asking for more.

He looked down at his pottage. He used his spoon to move the vegetables and herbs and other bits and pieces around in the hot water, and counted out the few tiny bits of

salted meat floating on top. He couldn't take a spoonful. He didn't even touch his bread. He was too nervous.

Roland had been so excited earlier. Now he was sad. He was sure that his father was about to say that he had chosen Shelby because he was older and stronger. Roland began to feel sick in the stomach. He wished he didn't have an older brother.

Mr. Wright was a short, squarely built man with big strong hands and wide shoulders. His nose was nearly flat and his forehead was scarred from being kicked by a horse years before, while trying to fit a shoe.

A weaker man would have been killed by the blow, but Mr. Wright had pulled himself off the floor, straightened his bleeding nose, grabbed back the horse's leg and finished fitting the shoe.

Mr. Wright now ran his right hand through his thick brown hair and cleared his throat.

"Boys, it has been an extraordinary day. It is, as Sir Gallawood said, a wonderful thing to save a king. And it is also a marvelous thing to know that a son of mine will enter the royal household."

Mr. Wright hardly ever showed his feelings, but today for the second time he couldn't help smiling a quiet, gentle smile.

"It will be a great distinction for

whichever son takes it up," he said. "I only wish your mother—God rest her soul—could be here to see it."

In another rare show of emotion, Mr. Wright went slightly red and his chin trembled. Mrs. Wright had died when Shelby was three years old and Roland was a few months short of two.

"She would have been so proud," said Mr. Wright. "Anyway, if the young man proves commendable as a page, he will become a squire at fourteen. Then, if he is worthy enough, in another five or six or perhaps seven years, well . . . as you heard, King John himself may pay to equip my son as a knight if he shows enough promise."

Roland couldn't quite remember that part of the officer-of-arms's speech. Nor could he remember hearing his father speak so many sentences in a row. He loved the sound of his father's strong, deep and slow voice.

Roland was always happy when his

father rested his big right hand on his shoulder or on the top of his head. He was sure that when his father was around he could never be scared of anything—even a real flying pig. Still, Roland could feel his stomach rumbling and turning. He looked across at Shelby, who seemed calm and confident. Their father started speaking again.

"As you know, boys, I love you both equally, so I have an unenviable decision to make. One of you will stay with me to learn my trade and take over this business. The other will start out on the path to being a knight.

"Both jobs will be hard work and there are no guarantees of success. The boy who becomes a page needs to know that the other pages will be from wealthy and powerful families. Only if you show yourself to be much, much better than them will you get anywhere. Only if you prove to be the strongest, the bravest and the most chivalrous will you succeed."

"I can do that," said Roland, who held up one of Nudge's paws as well as his own hand. "I can be good enough to be a knight."

"And I *will* be good enough to be a knight," snapped Shelby. He spoke so forcefully that Roland lost his grip on Nudge, causing him to fall tailfirst into Roland's pottage bowl.

"And as you know, Father," Shelby added, as Nudge thrashed and struggled and covered Roland's shirt in stew, "I'd be better at it than my younger brother."

"Now, now, boys," said Mr. Wright. "You must remember there are two jobs to be done. Of course a knight must be brave

and strong and true. But an armorer's job is just as significant, because if the knight doesn't have a good suit of armor, he can't be brave and strong and true for very long.

"And making things is one of the best things anyone can do. To take a lump of metal and turn it into a helmet, or a shield, or an entire suit of armor is a wonderful achievement."

Mr. Wright again ran his hand through his hair and continued. "Being an armorer is quite a bit safer than being a knight too, even if your chances of winning a fair maiden are lower."

"Who wants a fair maiden?" said Roland, scooping Nudge out of his pottage.

"Yes," said Shelby. "Girls never want to have sword fights or throw rocks in the river."

"Quiet," said Mr. Wright. "I have decided the only fair thing is to have a contest: a series of trials to see which of you is right for each job."

Roland glanced across at Shelby, who suddenly looked pale and upset.

"That's not fair," Shelby moaned. "I already work hard here at the forge for all of every day and Roland only has to do a bit of work each afternoon. I'm better than him at everything, and I'm the oldest, so I should be made the page. There shouldn't be a contest and—"

"He might work at the forge more than I do," interrupted Roland, "but in the mornings I look after the chickens and the pig, and I have to cut up the vegetables and go to the well.

"And Shelby might be the oldest but I'm just as good at fighting. That's what a knight has to do more of than anything else. And he's better at making things, and that's what an armorer has to do."

"What rot!" said Shelby, who was so angry that he threw his spoon at Roland. It hit Roland in the chest, right on the edge of his top pocket, where the pottage-soaked Nudge was now resting.

"Stop that, Shelby," said Mr. Wright as Nudge, whose tail had been squeezed by the flying spoon, let out a long squeak. "My mind is fixed. The contest will be in two days and you will both be set a series of tasks in the forge and in the field."

"But how will you choose a winner?" asked Roland.

"Nobody will win and nobody will lose," said Mr. Wright. "One of you will be chosen because I believe you will make the better armorer, and one of you will be chosen because I believe you will make the better knight."

"I want to be the better knight," said both boys at exactly the same time.

Six

A Knight's Advice

Roland sat on the village green, the large field near the forge, and rubbed Nudge's back gently with the middle finger of his right hand. Nudge wasn't pleased, though. He had another huge headache and wished Roland would give him some quality time on his own.

"I've done all my chores, Nudge, but I still have to go to work at the forge later," said Roland with a sigh. "So I've got only the rest of this morning to practice for the contest. But how can I practice when Father won't tell us what type of fighting we will be tested on?"

"   ," replied Nudge.

"Yes, that's it! You're right, or would be right if you ever talked. The contest simply has to include sword skills."

Roland jumped to his feet, threw an acorn against the nearest tree and slammed it with his wooden weapon as it bounced back. "But, Nudge, I haven't got anyone to fight. Unless . . ."

Nudge buried his nose under his paws. He wasn't going to be in a fight against Roland. He got hurt often enough when they were just being friends.

"All right, forget that," said Roland. "But tomorrow is the most important day of my life and I don't know what I should do."

Nudge removed one paw and looked up at Roland through his left eye.

"Here comes Jenny," Roland said

loudly. "I don't need to see her right now. I need to see someone who knows about being a better fighter. And look at her, she's skipping. Yuck!"

"You might be surprised what I know," said Jenny, who had heard Roland's rude comments as she tra-la-la-laed across the grass. "Anyway, didn't I hear Sir Gallawood tell you he would help? Surely Sir Gallawood could tell you what to do. You said he's the best, didn't you?"

Roland looked at Jenny and realized that girls weren't always completely, absolutely and utterly useless. Even girls who skipped.

"Flaming catapults, Jenny," said Roland, "that's a great idea!"

"Of course it's a great idea," said Jenny as she tra-la-la-laed away. "It's *my* idea."

Roland scooped up Nudge and flung him into his top pocket, which made Nudge's headache even worse. Roland started running as fast as he could toward

Gallawood Castle. He knew it was miles away and on top of the biggest hill in the district. It would take at least the rest of the morning to get there and back.

He had to hope that Sir Gallawood was home—and that he could give Roland some advice that made it worth using up his last free morning before the contest.

Roland ran down the potholed road as fast as his legs would take him. He stuck his bottom lip out and said to himself "Faster, faster, faster." For Nudge, each step was like being thrown high into the air, then being caught in a hammock. He felt his head was splitting.

Roland felt his head was splitting too. Still, he ran uphill as fast as he could under the morning sun, daydreaming of Sir Gallawood giving him a real suit of armor and a warhorse and teaching him to fight like a proper knight.

He daydreamed too of Shelby being terrified by his younger brother's new skills. In his mind he saw his sword slashing down at the speed of a diving hawk. He saw Shelby holding up his hands and yelling "I yield, I yield!"

When Roland was finally too tired to run anymore, he walked for a while. When he got his breath back, he ran again. When he lost it, he walked. He ran and walked, then walked and ran, then ran and walked, then walked and ran.

Finally Roland found himself at the end of the track, standing at the edge of a wide green moat.

On the other side of the water was a castle with stone walls as high as twenty men, and huge battlements on top. The black wooden drawbridge was pulled shut. Roland wondered what to do.

There were two archers on top of the gatehouse, but they were a long way away and Roland didn't feel he could yell that far. Anyway, he was almost too exhausted to speak.

Roland fell to his knees in disappointment. He'd come so far, and for something so important. Yet it looked like he'd wasted his time. He could have cried, but he was too exhausted.

"Young man," a voice suddenly blurted out, "what is your business here?"

Roland swung around to see a man in armor standing perfectly still under a little wooden shelter next to a tree.

"I'm here . . . ," said Roland, "I'm here
because . . . who are you?"

"I'm the advance guard," the man in
armor said, flicking up the visor on his helmet. He wore a bright red surcoat bearing
Sir Gallawood's family coat of arms.

"I'm here to protect the castle whenever the drawbridge comes down. And to

warn the defenders nice and early if anything else happens—like a little boy turns
up and threatens the safety of the castle."

"I'm not threatening the safety of the
castle," Roland said breathlessly. "I've just
come to see if Sir Gallawood is here."

"I'm not allowed to tell you whether he
is or he isn't," the advance guard said. "And
I couldn't let you inside, even if he was.
Which he may not be."

"But he knows me," said Roland.

"Nobody has mentioned to me that Sir
Gallawood is expecting a visitor," said the
advance guard. He snapped shut his visor
and returned his arms to his side.

"But, but, but," Roland panted, still
fighting to get enough air into his lungs.
"Sir Gallawood said I could call on him at
any time. It's very, very important."

"I still can't let you in," the advance
guard said loudly and sternly as he popped
his visor back up. "Not without a written
invitation. And even that wouldn't help,

because I can't read. Now you must let me get back to standing still."

The advance guard dropped his visor back down, as if to say that was the end of the discussion.

Roland dropped his eyes to the ground and hunched up his shoulders. "It's so important, it's just so important," he moaned. "You don't understand that it could change my whole life."

The advance guard stood silent and perfectly still. But then, suddenly, he lifted his visor just enough to whisper, "I am not allowed to let you in, or to tell you anything. The rules are the rules. But if you had been here a short while ago, you might have seen Sir Gallawood leave the castle for a calming walk. And you might have seen him walk down that track there."

"Thank you, thank you," Roland yelled as he started running in the direction the guard had pointed.

This track was even rougher than the one before. As Nudge bounced up and down, he became seasick and airsick and every other type of sick. But within a few moments Roland could see the tall and wide outline of his favorite knight up ahead.

"Sir Gallawood," Roland gasped and puffed as he reached the knight, who was dressed not in armor but in a long green tunic. "Sir Gallawood, Sir Gallawood . . . What do I need to know if I want to be just like you?"

"What?" the knight snapped. He reached for the handle of his sword, just in case this running, sweating, shouting boy was part of an ambush. "Who are you,

young man, and what do you mean by interrupting my walk?"

"I'm Roland, Roland Wright, one of Oliver Wright's sons. You know, Wright Armor?"

"Ahhhh! So you are," said Sir Gallawood in a much more gentle manner.

He took his hand off his sword. "Wright Armor," Sir Gallawood repeated, laughing loudly and giving Roland a friendly punch in the chest. The punch hit with an almighty *thwoomp* and although it missed Nudge by a hair's breadth, it almost bounced him out of Roland's shirt pocket. His headache was now even worse.

"I didn't recognize you, young Roland, with such a red face and so much sweat in your hair. So what can I do for you?"

"I've run all the way from the village, Sir Gallawood," Roland said, speaking so fast between breaths that Sir Gallawood had to squint his eyes and cup his hands behind his ears to work out what was being said. "I had to find you, Sir Gallawood. I'm in a contest tomorrow. Remember yesterday when we were told the King was taking one of my father's sons into his household. Well, my father is to choose which of us will make the better knight, and I'm going to fight in the contest just like you fight."

"Oh, I see," said Sir Gallawood as he planted another friendly punch on Roland's shoulder and kept walking. "We need to have a talk, then."

Once again, Sir Gallawood's friendly punch had almost flattened Roland.

Nudge, meanwhile, was quickly losing the will to live.

"So, young man," Sir Gallawood said as his long legs carried him along the rough dirt track so quickly that Roland had to jog to keep up. "What do you think you need to know before this contest?"

"Well, I need to know how to bash and crash and stab and slice and dice and pound," replied Roland, still rubbing his shoulder. "And I need to know how to smite people. All the great knights smite their enemies, so I need to know how to do that as well."

"Hmmm," said Sir Gallawood thoughtfully. "Being a knight, Master Roland, isn't only about fighting. Your father is a very clever man and I'm sure he knows that. So you'll have to show all the other knightly virtues in the contest. I trust you'll be judged on such things as honor, loyalty, good manners and chivalry."

"Oh," said Roland, still panting and

jogging and rubbing his shoulder. "I hadn't thought of that."

"And if I may offer another small piece of advice," Sir Gallawood said, smoothing his pointy black beard.

"You can offer a very big one," replied Roland. Despite how tired and sore he was, Roland was listening as carefully as he had ever listened to anything before.

"There is something, young Roland, that you always need to remember. The object of a contest is not to beat your opponent. The object is to be true to yourself. If you have done as well as you possibly can, and have behaved justly, nobly and never selfishly, then you have behaved like a good knight.

"And if you've behaved like a good knight, things will always work out for the best in the end."

Roland looked at the ground as he tried to take in Sir Gallawood's advice, and jog, and get the rest of his breath back at the same time.

"I will be true to myself tomorrow," Roland finally said.

Sir Gallawood smiled. Sadly, though, Roland wasn't sure exactly what being true to himself meant, or how he could find time to be true to himself when someone was attacking him with a sword. But he had made up his mind to follow the knight's advice.

"Something else, young man," added the knight.

"Yes, Sir Gallawood."

The knight held up his finger and stared straight into Roland's eyes.

"I have given you my time today. In return, you must promise me that you will behave like a good knight even if you are not the one your father chooses. If you uphold the virtues I spoke about—if you are just, noble and never selfish—you will not regret it, no matter what you do in life."

"Thank you, sir, thank you very much," said Roland as he turned to leave. "I promise you I will."

Roland could hear the church bells in

the distance. He had run out of time and now had to make it back to the forge. It was downhill, at least, but he'd have to run even faster than he'd run to get here.

"Not again," thought Nudge.

Seven

The Big Contest

Shelby and Roland stood in the forge with their father at first light on Saturday morning. The other workers were already banging and hammering. The furnace was roaring as David squeezed on the bellows.

"Remember, boys," Mr. Wright said, resting a hand on each son's shoulder. "I will be judging everything, and you must do your best in every challenge. The first challenge is to make something."

Mr. Wright pointed his sons to two separate workbenches, where he gave each a few pieces of wood, a box of nails and a selection of tools. There was a saw, a hammer, a wood file and a pair of pliers.

"I want you to each construct a wooden sword and shield," Mr. Wright said softly and deeply. "You must do it as well as you can and as quickly as you can. But there is something you need to bear in mind: we will go from here to the village green for the physical tests.

"When we do this, Shelby will use the sword and shield made by Roland, and Roland will have the sword and shield made by Shelby."

Roland thought about this for a moment. He knew that if he built a bad sword and shield, he would lose the first contest. But that might not be a bad thing. The boy who did better in the "making" contest was more likely to be chosen as the armorer.

And that wasn't all. Roland could also see that making a bad sword and shield would give him a better chance in any fighting, because it was Shelby who would have to use them. And the person who did better in fighting should be chosen as the knight. He started imagining that fight; he saw himself yelling "Attack!" and running at Shelby, ready to bash and crash and stab and slice and dice and pound and even smite.

Roland stopped daydreaming a few moments later, though. He realized Shelby had already started work, so soon he too was hammering and sawing and nailing the hard white wood. Roland soon felt long trails of sweat dripping down his face.

Roland was so absorbed in his task that he forgot about how long it was taking, or why he was doing it. He also forgot how Shelby was older than him, and had more practice at making things.

With his bottom lip stuck right out,

Roland was thinking about only one thing. He wanted to make the best sword and shield he possibly could. He knew he wasn't the greatest with a hammer and saw, but he never liked to do anything badly.

Anyway, as Sir Gallawood had told him, if Roland did as well as he possibly could, he would be behaving like a good knight.

If he gave Shelby a better sword and shield, Roland would just have to hope that, as the good knight said, it would all work out for the best.

"You have only a little longer, boys," warned Mr. Wright. "You must conclude shortly."

Roland used the wood file to smooth a few edges of his sword. He took the hammer and banged a couple more nails into the handle of the shield, to make it a little stronger.

He took one last look at his handiwork. It wasn't perfect but it was as good as he could do in such a short time. He then shouted, "Finished."

"Me too," yelled Shelby.

Mr. Wright grabbed up the swords and shields before either boy had a chance to look at what his brother had made.

"That was very illuminating," said Mr. Wright, but he didn't explain further. "Now we are moving to the village green."

They left the forge and were hit by the cool air outside. Even in midsummer it felt cold when you walked out of the forge.

When they reached the other side of the village square, Mr. Wright turned Roland and Shelby around. They walked back again. The same thing happened once more. On the third crossing, they saw Jenny's mother. She was carrying a bucket toward the well.

"How do you do, Mrs. Winterbottom?" said Shelby as he bowed before her.

Roland didn't want to be outdone. He made sure his father was watching before he bent even lower.

"Indeed, Mrs. Winterbottom," said Roland. "It is a pleasure to meet you so early on such a beautiful sunny day."

Mrs. Winterbottom looked down her pointy nose and made a huffing sound. "Dear, dear, dear." She had never seen Roland and Shelby behave like this.

"Mr. Wright," she said, "are you sure

your boys are well? Or is this how everyone behaves after a visit from the King's
officer-of-arms?"

Roland had leaned so far forward that
Nudge fell out of his shirt and onto the
ground, nose first. *Thump!* Suddenly

Nudge felt another thud as Roland's hand scooped him up and dropped him back in his top pocket.

"This is going to be a very long day," Nudge thought.

When Roland, Shelby and their father arrived at the village green, Mr. Nottingham, the mail-maker, was setting up a quintain.

The quintain was invented so knights could practice jousting. This quintain looked like the top half of a knight. It had an old breastplate and helmet attached. There was a shield in one arm and a big sandbag on the end of the other. The half-knight was mounted on a pole and could swing around.

"Do you know 'ow it works?" asked Mr. Nottingham. He was yawning because he had worked all though the night to build it. "You must charge toward it fast— *yaaawn,* excuse me—with a lance and 'it the shield.

"This is called 'tilting the quintain'— *yaaawn,* excuse me again. The quintain will swing around. If you don't get away quickly enough you'll be 'it 'ard by the 'eavy sandbag."

Mr. Wright took over.

"Normally you would tilt the quintain on a horse, but I've asked Mr. Nottingham to make it low so you boys can run at it. He's also brought you each a lance. But first I want you to sprint to the far hedge and then return . . . go, now!"

Roland wasn't expecting a footrace with so little warning. Shelby made a much quicker start and his long and strong legs carried him speedily. But Roland pumped his shorter legs as quickly as he could, and by the time they arrived at the hedge he had nearly caught up.

When they turned—Shelby leaving just as Roland was arriving—they collided. Roland was sure Shelby had swerved to get in his way. Roland barely managed to stay on his feet and had to try twice as hard to catch up again.

Right at the end, Roland dived to try to get ahead, but Shelby still beat him.

"The freckly redhead loses

again," laughed Shelby as Roland lay flat
on the ground, all the wind knocked out of
him—and out of Nudge.

There had been two tests: Roland had
no idea how he had done in the first one,
and had definitely lost the second. It wasn't
the start he needed.

Eight

Tilting the Quintain

Shelby ran toward the quintain with great speed. He struck the shield beautifully with the lance. There was an almighty crash and the half-knight spun around quickly.

But Shelby was smooth and fast, and the sandbag missed his back as he ran past.

"Your turn now, Roland," said Mr. Wright. "Remember that there are two aims—to hit the shield in the center, and to avoid the sandbag."

Roland put Nudge into the small cloth bag he always kept with him. He then placed Nudge carefully under a shady tree. Roland was worried. He was sure it wasn't possible to "tilt the quintain" better than his brother had just done it.

Roland nervously picked up the lance and ran toward the quintain as fast as he could. But he was running too quickly, and as he got close he started to lose his footing. He struck the shield well and there was a huge clanging, but Roland was stumbling and he could hear the sandbag spinning through the air toward him.

Being hit across the body by even a small sandbag hurts. And this was not a small sandbag. It lifted Roland off the ground and threw him three or four body lengths away, facedown into the grass.

Roland felt like a house had been dropped on him. Everything hurt, even his eyelids. For a couple of seconds Roland

was sure he would never move again. Then he clenched his fists, stuck out his bottom lip and painfully pulled himself off the ground.

"Did you learn anything?" asked Mr. Wright.

"Yes, I should close my mouth when I am heading for the ground face-first," said Roland, spitting out blades of grass.

The brothers each had to tilt the quintain a second time. Shelby again struck the shield perfectly and managed to get away before being hit by the sandbag.

When it was Roland's second turn, every step hurt. Even holding the lance made his arms ache. When he struck the shield right in the center he knew he was too sore to run away quickly enough. Instead he dropped straight to the ground and felt the sandbag pass over his back, just missing him.

The sandbag passed over Roland three times before it stopped swinging. He then felt safe enough to slowly pull himself off the grass. He knew his father said there were two aims: to hit the shield and avoid the sandbag. He had done it this time, even if it wasn't in the normal way. Shelby, though, had done it twice, so had clearly won the quintain competition too.

Village green score: Shelby 2, Roland 0.

"Are you sure you are well enough to continue, Roland?" asked Mr. Wright.

"Of course," Roland replied as cheerfully as he could. But everything still ached.

It was time for archery, which at least gave Roland's bruises and sore bones a little time to settle down.

Roland put Nudge back into his top pocket for good luck. "We have to do this well, Nudge," he whispered, "or it will be Shelby Wright—future knight."

Mr. Wright handed each boy a bow and a quiver with four arrows in it. Neither had used a real bow and arrow before. Although the target looked close, Shelby missed it completely with his first shot. So did Roland. Shooting arrows wasn't as easy as it looked. Even drawing back the bow-string was hard work.

With his second shot, Shelby sent his arrow into the target, though only on the outer ring. Roland did the same. Shelby's third shot was excellent, making it inside the first ring. Then Roland surprised everyone by hitting the black circle in the center.

"Flaming catapults, Nudge," he shouted out. "We've done it. It's a bull's-eye."

They each had one arrow left. Shelby lined up his final shot, knowing he needed a bull's-eye to have a chance of winning. But he didn't look worried. He calmly turned to his brother and said, "Watch this, Roland Wright—future *armorer*."

But Shelby was too relaxed and suddenly the fingers of his right hand slipped off before he had properly drawn back the bowstring. The arrow fell to his feet.

"That wasn't my real go," said Shelby. He quickly picked up the arrow. "I can take that shot again, can't I, Father?"

"Perhaps," said Mr. Wright. "That's a decision for Roland."

Roland looked at the ground. What should he do? He needed to win a contest at the village green. But was it a real victory if he won by anything other than being better?

Sir Gallawood had said Roland needed to be just and noble. But right now Roland wasn't sure he could afford to be.

Roland looked down at Nudge, closed his eyes, took a deep breath, then looked at Nudge again. What should he do? Nudge twitched his whiskers, rubbed his black eyes and stared up at Roland. "Yes," thought Roland, "you're right again, Nudge."

"Shelby," Roland said, "of course you can have another shot."

Shelby concentrated much harder this time and sent his arrow whistling right into the center of the target, less than a finger space away from Roland's last arrow.

"Aha!" yelled Shelby. "A bull's-eye for me too."

Roland couldn't believe it. His kindness had given Shelby a bull's-eye—and Shelby hadn't even said thank you. With his last shot, Roland needed another bull's-eye to stay ahead.

Roland was shaking with nerves as he prepared to shoot. If he could win the archery competition, the village green score would be two to Shelby and one to Roland. That meant if Roland had built the best weapons at the forge, the overall score would be two all. It might all come down to the final sword fight.

But first, Roland had to hit the target. He drew back the bowstring with all his strength. His arms still hurt. So did his eyelids. And his ears and his chest and his legs.

"Wish me luck, Nudge," he whispered to his top pocket. Roland opened his eyes as widely as he could, jutted out his bottom lip and finally released.

There was a loud whooshing noise. From the moment the arrow left his bow, Roland knew it was the best thing he had done all day. He watched the arrow sail, almost in slow motion, from the tips of his fingers right into the center of the bull's-eye.

It landed with a *thwack* right between the two arrows that had already been shot into the little black circle.

"We did it, Nudge. We did it!" Roland sighed with enormous relief. "Now I think I should put you back in the bag for the sword fight."

"I think so too," thought Nudge.

Nine

The Sword Fight

The fight had begun and Roland was putting in the biggest effort of his life. He was bashing and crashing and stabbing and slicing and dicing and pounding—and maybe even smiting as well. Again and again, Roland swung his wooden sword as hard as he could, hitting Shelby clean across the face.

Normally Roland wouldn't hit his brother, or anyone else, in the face.

But this was different—Mr. Wright had

supplied helmets for them both. They even had metal breastplates strapped on with leather to protect their bodies.

The sound of the wooden sword hitting the steel helmet made a horrible noise for those outside. It was even worse inside Shelby's helmet. As Shelby stood there vibrating like a dinner gong, Roland thrust hard with his sword into his breastplate. And although Roland was hitting Shelby again and again, Shelby was hardly ever hitting his younger brother.

Roland imagined the little acorn bouncing left or right off the curved wall of the well. His sword flew this way and that at almost lightning speed. Roland stabbed Shelby's breastplate once, twice, three times. Each was harder than the one before. Roland knew if he wanted to be a knight, this might be his last chance.

"Take that, Sir Shelby," he yelled in delight. With the fourth powerful thrust, Roland heard a crunch. He looked down and saw the end of his sword break off and fall to the ground. It was not a good sword. The grip was rough and the cross-guard that was meant to protect his hand was not attached properly.

The shield Roland was using was small too, and its handle was hard to hold tightly.

Roland wasn't going to blame his equipment. He had often heard his father say "A bad tradesman blames his tools." Roland didn't want to be a bad tradesman. He wanted to be a good knight. In all the tasks his father had set them, he had stuck out his bottom lip and tried harder than he had ever tried before. In the final fight, everything seemed to be going well right up until the moment when his sword broke in half.

Shelby, with a bigger shield and a longer, better-made sword, at once saw his chance. He hit Roland across the helmet.

The noise was horrible and Roland knew his face was going to come up in bruises. But there was little he could do. He didn't have enough reach with his broken sword. His body still hurt from being hit by the sandbag. And he was as tired as he had ever been in his life.

He felt Shelby's sword crash against his helmet. Twice, thrice, four times.

Roland's whole body was shaking now with the clanging of the sword on his helmet. When the blows stopped, it was only because Shelby had turned around to make sure that their father was seeing how well he was now doing.

For a few seconds Roland had the chance to attack his brother from behind. Roland's wooden sword was broken and so was sharper and more dangerous. And there was no armor on Shelby's back.

With his ears still ringing, Roland lifted his weapon slightly. But Sir Gallawood's words came straight back to him. "The object is to be true to yourself."

Roland at last knew what being true to

himself meant. He wasn't a dirty fighter. He knew he wasn't a cheat. He had to behave like a good knight.

At that moment, Shelby bent his knees, lifted his sword and swung it around with frightening speed. Roland quickly spun to get out of the way, but Shelby's sword was moving too fast. And because Roland had turned around, the sword slashed not across his breastplate but his unprotected back.

It was a terrible blow. It felt like a red-hot strip of steel had been pressed against Roland's skin. He fell to the ground face-first in agony. He rolled onto his back, hoping the softness of the grass would stop the pain. Shelby stood above him, ready to strike the final blow.

"Stop, stop, stop," yelled Mr. Wright. "I think that's it."

"No," groaned Roland in a tiny voice. "I can get up."

With that, Roland painfully wriggled sideways. Shelby stabbed the grass where

Roland had been only a split second earlier. Roland pulled himself to his feet and,
despite everything, held on to what was
left of his sword. Shelby pulled his own
sword out of the ground. He raced back
toward Roland and swung it as hard as he
could.

Roland held out his shield and stopped
the blow, but the shield broke in two and

fell to the ground. The hand that was holding it now stung horribly.

Roland knew it was now or never. He stuck out his bottom lip and raced at Shelby with a series of swings and swipes. He found an opening and drove what was left of his sword into Shelby's breastplate. It was a fine thrust. But the second the broken wooden sword hit the steel, the sword smashed into dozens of tiny pieces.

There was nothing more Roland could do. He had no sword, he had no shield and his back was throbbing. Roland fell to one knee, held his hands in the air and said with a small, sad voice, "I yield. You were too good for me, Sir Shelby. Well done."

"I told you I was the best," said Shelby. "We never needed a contest."

When Roland took off his helmet, his red hair looked black because of all the sweat, and his freckles were all joined together by dirt.

Shelby removed his helmet and

straightened his blond hair with his hand. He tried to stop puffing and panting. Roland had put up a terrific fight, but Shelby didn't want anyone to think it had been close. He wanted it to look like beating his brother had been no trouble at all.

Mr. Wright called them over.

"I have acquired a great deal of knowledge watching you two today. I will give you my decision after Mass tomorrow."

That night, an exhausted Roland blew out his candle and put his head down on his straw bed. Above the sound of the chickens next to the door and the pig under the table, and the summer rain on the roof, he could still hear Shelby breathing. It seemed to be happy, light breathing. Roland was sure Shelby must be smiling.

"You're going to be chosen tomorrow," Roland finally said. Shelby said nothing.

Roland stared up at the blackness and felt very, very sad. A wonderful chance had been offered to him, the chance to be a knight. It was an opportunity that would come to a boy like him only once in a hundred lifetimes. Yet Roland had lost the "fighting" part and had won the "making" part.

"Shelby was right," he whispered to

Nudge, who was lying in a small elm-wood box next to the bed. "Roland Wright—future armorer. It doesn't even sound good."

Roland tried hard to feel happy for Shelby. Even if he was no longer going to be a real knight, Roland had made a promise to Sir Gallawood.

No matter what happened, Roland had to be noble and generous. He had to tell himself that he was sure that Shelby would be a good page, a good squire and, in time, a good knight.

There was only one thing that stopped Roland bursting into tears. He knew he couldn't have tried any harder.

Ten

One to the Castle

"**I** have reached my decision," said Mr. Wright as they arrived back home from Sunday Mass. It had been hard for Roland to drag his bruised body out of bed, and even harder for him to stand in the church and look at the old stained-glass windows. They showed the bravest knights in the district heading for the Holy Land.

Roland now looked into Nudge's black eyes. He had to. He couldn't look up at his father, or across at Shelby. He was sure his older brother was about to be given the best news of his life.

But Nudge didn't look worried at all. He was back to his usual self, sniffing the air and grabbing anything that took his fancy so he could chew on it.

"I observed many things yesterday that pleased me," said Mr. Wright as he shooed away the chickens and leaned against the small table wedged between the beds. "You both competed well and bravely, and listened to instructions and were mostly polite."

"I saw Shelby run beautifully to win the sprint. I saw him tilt the quintain as if he had been doing it for years.

"Shelby was the first to behave with chivalry toward Mrs. Winterbottom, too. And although Shelby didn't win the archery, he came back after a problem and scored a bull's-eye."

Roland now glanced across at his brother. Shelby was staring straight up at their father. His eyes were glinting as Mr. Wright listed the things his elder son had done well. Roland was sure his father had said more in the past few days than in all the rest of his life.

"As for Roland," Mr. Wright continued, "I saw him having problems with his sword and shield in the fight, but he never once complained. That shows self-reliance. He was prepared to do the best with what he was given.

"And I saw Roland make a superior sword and shield. By doing this he showed he would be a good tradesman."

Roland had smiled broadly when his father praised his sword fighting, but now he was shaking. He didn't want to be a good tradesman, or even a terrible one. He wanted to be a knight. He wanted to yell this out at the top of his voice but his mouth was dry and no words would come out.

"But in making a good sword and shield," said Mr. Wright, "Roland showed not only that he would be a good trades-man."

Mr. Wright looked down at his younger son. "Roland, you showed you are generous and gallant. You made the better sword and shield even though you knew your brother would be the one to use them.

"And you let Shelby take an extra shot in the archery."

Mr. Wright paused for what seemed like forever. It was probably only a few short moments. "Being generous and gallant," he said, "are virtues that would make a good knight."

Shelby gasped. Maybe it wasn't as clearcut as it first seemed, thought Roland. Maybe, just maybe, he still had a chance.

"And, Roland, you got up from that heavy knock from the quintain, when I was sure you wouldn't be able to, and again during the sword fight. And you were noble in defeat, saying 'Well done' to Shelby, the winner.

"On the other hand, Shelby, you fought skillfully too. You didn't give up even when Roland started so strongly."

Mr. Wright looked at the two boys, then

put his big right hand on Shelby's shoulder.

"I know how talented you are, Shelby. I see you working at the forge every day and I am almost always proud of you. But that's how I know you could have made a better sword and shield for your brother. That was a disappointment.

"You also need to behave better when you win. Nobody likes a winner who crows about it, or is rude to the people he beats. That's as bad as someone who doesn't win and then complains that the contest wasn't fair.

"Then again, Shelby, you won more events in the contest than Roland."

Both boys were now staring at the ground. Neither had a clue what their father had decided. Roland wished his father would put his hand on his shoulder, if only to stop him shivering with nerves.

"Choosing which of you would be the armorer and which would be the page was never going to be an easy decision. But after considering everything, I have decided that my older son, Shelby . . ."

Both boys breathed in as they waited for the words that would follow. Roland covered his eyes. He was as tense as he had ever been in his life. Only Nudge seemed to be breathing normally as Mr. Wright continued his long sentence.

". . . who is talented and intelligent and should be proud of almost all his efforts yesterday, will be . . ."

There was a complete silence in the room. Roland wondered if his heart had stopped beating.

". . . trained here in the forge as an armorer. And I am sure that Shelby will eventually become the best armorer in the country."

Nudge squeaked loudly as Roland sat, stunned.

"That means," Mr. Wright continued, "that Roland will be sent to the castle to work in the royal household. Just as I believe in Shelby's talents, I believe Roland has what it takes to be very good at what he does."

The room fell silent again while Roland took in the news. He had done it, and not in the way he expected. Roland had won the competition not by beating his opponent but by being noble and generous and just and true to himself.

He could have stopped Shelby having an extra shot in the archery, but he didn't. He could have used dirty tactics in the sword fight, but he had decided against it.

Roland had behaved like a good knight and, just as Sir Gallawood had said, things had worked out for the best.

Roland jumped up and threw Nudge in the air with joy.

"Flaming catapults," Roland screamed as he ran across the dirt floor of the house and gave his father the biggest hug he could. "I really am Roland Wright, future knight."

"Yes," said his father, "but you forgot about Nudge. You are lucky your brother caught him."

Roland turned back to grab Nudge, who gave him a very dirty look.

"One more thing, Roland," said Mr. Wright, dropping his big right hand onto his son's shoulder. "You impressed me greatly. Congratulations. I'm sure I won't regret my decision, but I don't want you to think you are too good. You have a lot to learn."

"Yes, Father," said Roland softly. Roland suddenly realized that his victory was Shelby's loss. He turned around and looked at his brother, who was sitting on the edge of his bed. Shelby was red in the face and nearly in tears.

Roland felt sorry for Shelby. Sure, Shelby had been mean and selfish and unfair. But older brothers are always mean and selfish and unfair, so Shelby was only doing his job. Roland was glad he had an older brother. He was glad his older brother was Shelby.

"I wish we could both be pages," Roland said, putting his arm around his

brother's neck. "In time I will become a knight, no matter how hard I have to work at it. When I do, I will wear your armor. It will be the best armor in the world, and we are both going to make our father proud.

"Oh, and thanks, Shelby, for catching Nudge."

Shelby, with a lone tear running down his cheek, looked at his younger brother.

"I hope we can make him proud, Roland. When we lay in bed last night I heard you say I was going to win. I didn't say anything. I wanted to agree with you, but I was worried. I had won more events but I still knew something was wrong.

"Father was clever to test us on more things than I realized we were being tested on. I wanted to win each event so much that I forgot about being fair and generous, and all the other things that a good knight must be."

Roland gave his older brother one last squeeze around the neck and walked outside into the sunshine. He didn't feel like he was walking on a dirt track. He felt like he was walking on the clouds.

Roland saw Jenny skipping down the trail toward him. He couldn't help but smile.

"You were right, Jenny, you were right. Sir Gallawood told me what to do—and I did it and I won!"

"Of course I was right," Jenny said. She skipped on by toward her own house at the edge of the wood.

Roland lifted Nudge onto his shoulder and climbed his favorite oak tree. They both looked out over the thatched roofs of the houses, across the cornfields to Sir Gallawood's castle high on the hill, and the cloudless blue sky beyond.

"Roland Wright," the small redheaded boy repeated to his littlest friend. "Roland Wright, future knight."

"   ," added Nudge happily.

Acknowledgments

The author would like to thank two sets of brothers who test-drove the manuscript: William and James Davis, and Lachlan and Joshua Coady. Also a big thank-you to Carolyn Walsh, whose judgment was always spot-on; Sharon "No Relation" Davis (the Grovedale West Primary School wonder librarian); my ever-helpful parents, Pedr and Dolores; Debbie Vermes; Graham Harman; and editors Jessica Dettmann and Kimberley Bennett.

Lastly, thanks to executive editors on two continents—Zoe Walton and Françoise Bui—who made possible my escape into a medieval world, and to Gregory Rogers for bringing Roland's story to life so wonderfully with his illustrations.

About the Author

Tony Davis has always worked with words. He has been a book publisher, a magazine editor, and a newspaper writer. In recent years he has been a full-time book author—his most difficult but exciting job yet.

Tony has long been interested in knights and armor, and the legends and stories of the Middle Ages. His enthusiasm for the period comes through clearly in the world of Roland Wright.

When he is not putting words on paper (or screens), Tony is playing football or cricket in the backyard with his three sons, strumming a guitar, reading, hiking, or listening to music on his stereo, iPod, or hand-cranked 78-rpm record player.

About the Illustrator

Gregory Rogers studied fine art at the Queensland College of Art in Australia and has illustrated a large number of educational and trade children's picture books. He won the Kate Greenaway Medal for his illustrations in *Way Home*.

His first wordless picture book, *The Boy, The Bear, The Baron, The Bard*, was selected as one of the *New York Times* Ten Best Illustrated Children's Books of the Year and received numerous other awards and nominations. He also illustrated *Midsummer Knight*, the companion to *The Boy, The Bear, The Baron, The Bard*.

Coming Soon

Roland Wright's knightly adventures continue in

Roland Wright #2
Brand-New Page

IIt's really happened—Roland Wright is joining the royal household at Twofold Castle as a brand-new page! This is his big chance to impress the King and his knights.

But Roland encounters a few difficulties:

1. The Queen hates mice, so it looks as if Nudge, Roland's pet mouse, can't stay.

2. There's an older page who makes sure poor boys like Roland get sent home in disgrace.

3. A huge, tusked animal is on the loose. . . .

If things don't improve, Roland's dream of being a knight could be over in a day.

TURN THE PAGE TO READ CHAPTER ONE

One

Twofold Castle

"**F**laming catapults, Nudge, have you ever seen such a castle?"

The correct answer was "no." But because Nudge was a small white mouse, he couldn't say it.

Even if he could, the ten-year-old— well, almost-ten-year-old—redheaded boy who had asked the question was far too excited to wait for an answer.

"Imagine if there was a siege," Roland said as the pair looked up at King John's castle, an enormous stone fortress covering the entire top of the hill.

"Can't you just see hundreds of soldiers protecting the King, Nudge? Hundreds of archers shooting arrows from the battlements down onto the attackers . . . and soldiers pouring boiling oil on men charging at the drawbridge with a battering ram . . . and gallant knights swinging broadswords atop warhorses covered with shining armor."

As it turned out, Nudge couldn't see any of that. He stood on Roland's shoulder, sniffed the air with his pink nose and continued to look around. All he could see was a castle so quiet and peaceful it seemed almost to be sleeping under the blue summer sky. Nudge could hear birds singing and the sound of the wind rustling the leaves in the trees.

Roland, however, could hear the whoosh of spears, the shouting of soldiers, the snorting of horses waiting to charge.

He could smell flaming arrows hitting the wet leather that had been strung up to protect the siege towers from fire. He could feel the castle shuddering as boulders were slung into the walls by the most powerful catapult of all, the trebuchet.

Mind you, Roland had been daydreaming about such things for most of the two days he and his small group had been traveling. When Roland wasn't daydreaming, he was talking about all the things he would do and learn as a new page at the King's castle.

"I'll go to tournaments and see real jousting," he said to his taller, blond-haired brother, Shelby, as they walked along. "And I'll learn to ride horses and to hunt with falcons. I'm the luckiest boy in the whole world."

"You certainly are," said Shelby, still a little sad that his younger brother had been chosen ahead of him. "But I know you'll make the most of it."

"And Father," said Roland, "I'm going to be the best page, then the best squire, then the best knight. I know if I try hard enough I can be, and you'll be so proud of me. Especially when I wear armor made by you."

"I have abundant faith in you, Roland," said his father, flicking back his thick brown hair and kindly pretending that he hadn't heard Roland say the same thing again and again for two whole days. "You can do anything if you set your mind to it, son. You've already demonstrated that."

There was someone else Roland spoke to on the long journey to the King's castle from the small village where the Wright family lived: Sir Gallawood. He had offered to travel with the Wrights, as it could be a dangerous business walking through the woods in the year 1409. It could be dangerous doing many other things six centuries ago too, so it was always handy to take a knight in armor along with you.

Roland was on the lookout for thieves or bandits or poachers—and always a little disappointed when he didn't see any.

"Sir Gallawood, please tell me more about King John . . . and his castle," said Roland as he walked alongside the knight's horse.

"Well, young Roland," said Sir Gallawood, "it's called Twofold Castle.

That's because it has double walls to make it even safer from attack. And there are many, many pages there, most of them sons of the most important men in the country." He let out a hearty laugh. "Well, the sons of the men who *think* they are the most important in the country."

Sir Gallawood looked down at Roland with a more serious expression. "Twofold Castle is a magnificent place. The finest horses are there, and the best squires and of course the bravest, most talented knights. I personally promised the King I would bring you safely to his castle to start your new life as a page."

"You've met the King!" Roland cried with glee.

"Yes, I—" Sir Gallawood started, but he was straightaway interrupted by Roland.

"Flaming catapults, Sir Gallawood, that's so exciting. I can't think of anything more wonderful than meeting the King, except fighting in a battle alongside him. What is he like?"

"King John is a fair and just man," said Sir Gallawood. "And now he has given you a chance that almost never comes to boys who aren't from noble families. Always remember: being a page is the first step to being a knight, but it is also about serving King John and his court. It will be a great honor to do that. You are a very lucky boy."

Sir Gallawood was right. Roland knew how fortunate he was. It wasn't just that the King's life had been saved by a suit of armor made by Roland's father. Nor was it that the King had offered to take in one of the armorer's sons as a way of saying thank you. The truly remarkable thing was that Roland had been chosen ahead of his brother, Shelby, who was already eleven.

Roland looked up at the walls and turrets of Twofold Castle and cried out, "We're here, Nudge! We're here!"

But sitting up on that huge hill, the castle was still half an afternoon's walk away. That was enough time for Roland to tell his father several more times that he was going to be the best page, then the best squire and then the best knight. It was also enough time to ask Sir Gallawood another thirty questions about life in a castle. And to daydream some more too.

When the small group finally arrived at the edge of the green moat that surrounded Twofold Castle, a sentry shouted from the top of the gatehouse. The large black drawbridge soon dropped and a man on a beautiful white horse rode out to meet the newcomers.

"So, this is the leave-taking," sighed Roland's father.

"Ah, Sir Gallawood," said the man on the white horse, ignoring the others. His voice sounded like a big, rusty hinge being opened. It echoed around the hills.

"Yes, Constable," said Sir Gallawood, "I present to you a small and thin, but very, very brave young boy named Roland Wright."

Sir Gallawood dismounted and put his hand on Roland's shoulder. "And Roland, I present to you the King's constable, who is in charge of running the castle."

The constable was a mountain of a man. He wore a bright red surcoat with the royal crest on the front. He had the biggest, blackest mustache Roland had ever seen. His head was completely bald and shiny, but his eyebrows were almost as big, black and bushy as his mustache.

Roland couldn't see his eyes or his mouth through all the hair.

"I'm pleased to meet you, Sir Constable," Roland said, wondering where to look.

"Just call me Constable, and always do exactly as I tell you," came the reply from somewhere under the mustache. The voice was so low and creaky it made Roland's ears ache. "Now, let's hurry along."

Roland realized that after all the hours of traveling there wasn't going to be time to say goodbye properly. The constable was in a hurry, and Roland had to do exactly as he was told.

"Bye, Father, bye, Shelby," he blurted as the constable grabbed him by one arm, and Sir Gallawood grabbed him by the other, then helped prop him on the back of the constable's horse.

"We won't see you for at least a year, but we are confident you'll make us proud, son," Oliver Wright called as Roland found himself galloping across the drawbridge.

Roland was through the double walls of Twofold Castle and into the castle yard before he had time to wipe away the tears that were forming in his eyes. He didn't even look around at his new home. He just thought about how he no longer had his father and his brother by his side. The only friend at hand was Nudge, now safely in his small elm-wood box inside Roland's sack.

"Do you know what is expected of you

here, young man?" asked the constable loudly as he leapt off the horse and watched Roland fumble his way out of the saddle.

"Not completely," said Roland, who was still in shock and trying very hard to dry his eyes with his handkerchief while pretending to blow his nose. "But I am very keen to learn. I'm going to be the greatest knight in the world."

"They all say that," the constable rasped. "But most pages never even become squires, let alone knights. Some are sent home in the first week because they aren't right for the job.

"The only thing expected of you here, young Roland, is that you do exactly as you are told, and you speak to your betters only when asked a question. Do you understand that?"

"Yes, sir. I mean, yes, constable."

"As we are busy because of the elephant, I'm going to ask—"

"The elephant?" Excitement raced back

into Roland's voice, but it quickly disappeared. The constable's huge eyebrows quivered and his shiny bald head reddened.

"I did not ask a question," he snapped. "You certainly have a lot to learn about how we do things here, young man."

At that point a boy ran up to the center of the courtyard where Roland and the constable were standing. He was nine or ten years old and was wearing the royal page uniform—a tunic with large red and blue squares, pulled tight by a thick black leather belt. The boy had curly yellow hair—the longest hair on a young boy Roland had ever seen.

"Humphrey," said the constable. "I want

you to take young Roland to his room so he can put his things down. Then I want you to look after him until it's time for him to join in the chores."

"Yes, constable, yes, constable." The boy seemed almost to dance as he talked—it was as if he couldn't stand still. Roland, who often had "hunches," decided straightaway that this boy with the long straw-colored hair was going to be a friend.

As the constable remounted his horse and rode away, Humphrey turned to Roland and smiled.

"Welcome to Twofold Castle, to Twofold Castle. We've all heard about you—the son of the famous armorer, the famous armorer. You are so lucky to be here right now. Tomorrow is going to be the most exciting day, the most exciting day for years."